STAR OF THE WEEK

A Story of Love,
Adoption,
and Brownies
With Sprinkles

STAR OF THE

A Story of Love, Adoption, an

story by **DARLENE FRIEDMAN**

illustrations by **ROGER ROTH**

The Bowen Press

An Imprint of HarperCollinsPublishers

WEEK

Brownies with Sprinkles

This book is dedicated to our amazing daughter, Eden. You are the light and love of our lives.

Also, to the memory of Howard J. Friedman (we miss you, Dad), and to all the wonderful people who enrich our lives—the few who are represented in this book and the many others who are not.

Special thanks to our editor, Anne Hoppe, for her faith in this project.

—D.F. and R.R.

Crayon image on page 26 provided by Eden Yi Friedman Roth.

Star of the Week: A Story of Love, Adoption, and Brownies with Sprinkles
Text copyright © 2009 by Darlene Friedman   Illustrations copyright © 2009 by Roger Roth

Library of Congress Cataloging-in-Publication Data is available.
ISBN 978-0-06-114136-2 (trade bdg.) — ISBN 978-0-06-114137-9 (lib. bdg.)

Typography by Jeanne L. Hogle
1 2 3 4 5 6 7 8 9 10
❖
First Edition

Hi. My name is Cassidy-Li. I am six years old. I'm in kindergarten at Buena Vista Elementary and my teacher is Mrs. Lerman. Next week, it's my turn to be Star of the Week.

Star of the Week is when you bring in a poster that's all about YOU. You get to do special things too, like bringing in a snack for the class. Mom and I are baking brownies and I'm going to decorate them with sprinkles.

It's time to get started on my poster.

I look through my special memory box.

This photo was taken in China, where I was born. My mom and dad adopted me from there when I was a baby.

I have a goofy headband on. Mom and Dad look so happy. I look happy too.

This is my friend Shirley and me at the dollar store. She was the first person to meet me in America. She picked us up at the airport. I was tired from the long trip and slept in the car.

Me and Shirley

Rebeka is my cousin, but we are more like sisters.

She moved far away with her mom. I miss her a lot.

Rebeka comes to visit during the summer.

Grandma Cate and Grandpa Bill

Grandma Bell and Grandpa Harry

I dig through the box and find a bunch more photos.

My cousins Josh and Ian

Soccer

Piano lessons

Chinese school

Sleepover!

Elizabeth is my best friend. We go to Chinese school every
Saturday. We learn songs and dance wearing beautiful
Chinese dresses.

My other best friend is Miranda. We met at preschool. She has a brother, Charles. Sometimes he's a pain.

These are my Chinese "cousins." We were adopted from the same orphanage. Every fall, we have a reunion.

I have lots of pets.

Diamond

Sparkles

Wolfie

Wolfie sleeps with me at night.

Sometimes he eats my toys.

My poster is almost done. But something is missing.

I don't have any photos of my birthparents.

I think about my birthparents a lot. Sometimes I miss them. I was born to them. I am a part of them, and they are a part of me.

I wonder what they look like. Are they nice? Where do they live?

Why couldn't they keep me? Do they miss me like I miss them?

Mom, Dad, and I have talked about all the reasons people can't take care of their babies.

They might be very poor, or maybe too young.

People like Mom and Dad adopt babies who need a family to take care of them. Mom says families are families and it doesn't matter how they're formed.

I love my parents, but I'm sad about my birthparents. Dad says our family loves my birthparents very much even though we'll never know them.

I decide to draw a picture of my birthparents for my poster.

I glue dragonflies, hearts, and stars all around the pictures.

My poster is done.

I am excited about tomorrow, but also a little nervous.
I wonder if my friends will ask a lot of questions about
my birthparents and adoption. I don't like to talk about it
sometimes. Mom and Dad say I can tell people it's private
if I want to.

The next morning, I get dressed quicker than usual. I don't want to be late for my big day! Dad and Wolfie walk me to school. I think they're excited too.

Mrs. Lerman tells everyone to gather round.

Then I show my poster.

Everyone claps when I am done. A few kids give me high fives. My name is Cassidy-Li, and I am a star.